If YOU BELIEVE IN Me

NATALIE J. DAMSCHRODER

Entangled Publishing, LLC
2614 South Timberline Road
Suite 109
Fort Collins, CO 80525
Visit our website at www.entangledpublishing.com.

Select Contemporary is an imprint of Entangled Publishing, LLC.

Edited by Kerri-Leigh Grady
Cover design by LJ Anderson
Cover art from 123RF

Manufactured in the United States of America

First Edition December 2012

This story is dedicated to all of the men and women who have served this country, with special thanks to the following:

My father and stepmother, Sergeant Charles Jacobus and Sergeant Patricia Jacobus, United States Air Force (Honorably Discharged)

My brother, Spc Peter Jacobus, United States Army

My "little" cousin DJ, Army Spc David S. Stelmat, killed in action while serving as a medic in Iraq during Operation Iraqi Freedom

and United States Air Force Colonel Marc DiPaolo, extended family

Huge thanks to my editor, Kerri-Leigh Grady, for telling me everything I got wrong, and to her husband CDR Jody Grady for feeding her all the details we needed to make it as close to "right" as we could and still do what I wanted to do.

Chapter One

Amber hummed a Christmas carol into the frigid evening air, her boots thudding on the snow-dusted steps of the Rikers' front porch. She shifted the grocery bag to her left arm to unlock the door and grunted when her tote slid off her right shoulder. She could almost hear Kale's chuckle as he teased her for not making two trips to the car, and the longing that swelled her throat killed the desire to sing.

She swallowed hard and tugged off her mitten, catching the keys before they fell. Kale's parents were still at work, but she'd wanted a head start making their "traditional" week-before-the-holiday dinner—if two years in a row could be considered a tradition. They might not have heard from Kale for six months, but if they *were* able to talk to him wherever he was stationed right now, she didn't want to be tied to the stove.

Plus, the more she had ready before they got home, the more she could relax with the couple that had become her surrogate parents in the last couple of years. She shivered at a gust of wind, slid the key into the deadbolt, and paused. *If it turns without sticking, he's safe and coming home to us.*

Her spirits lifted when it did, the song returning with a new lilt. She "br-rrr"ed and quickly closed the door behind her, careful to keep her feet on the woven runner while she toed off her boots. Halfway through, she froze, her humming fading into silence. Something was wrong.

The Rikers always had their artificial tree up by today, exactly one week before Christmas. But that corner of the room stood empty and shadowed. No lights twinkled along the mantle. Her nose wrinkled at the house's chill staleness. Even when they were at work, the house always greeted her with scents of fresh pine from the boughs climbing the banister and spice from clove-studded oranges and gingerbread candles. Why hadn't they decorated yet?

She tried to shrug off her uneasiness and headed toward the kitchen. Hopefully, no one was sick. She hadn't talked to them in a couple of days, but they would have told her to reschedule if something had come up. Okay, they were humoring her a little. She knew her insistence on doing everything the same way wouldn't guarantee anything. Kale had been here the first year she cooked chicken marsala for him and his parents. Last year, he'd been able to videoconference with them, which was better than nothing. *This year will be nothing, and next year—*

Amber slammed the door shut on that well-traveled thought path, but her unease grew. The house was so still, she kept glancing over her shoulder at the echo from her own footsteps.

She snapped on the radio to keep her company and began emptying the bag of groceries. Chicken, pasta, mushrooms, butter, scallions… They'd have flour and all the spices already. But dammit, she'd forgotten the wine in her car.

Halfway back to the front door, she spotted the suitcases at the foot of the stairs. What were those doing there? The Rikers never went anywhere during the holidays.

Maybe the baggage was empty. She hurried over, hating the dread that grew with every step. They could have just been cleaning out closets or something, planning to move the bags up to the attic when they brought down the holiday decorations. She yanked at the biggest one, ready for it to pop up off the floor. Pain snapped through her shoulder. It was full. Heavy. She blinked back flashing lights in her peripheral vision and sank down on the lowest stair, clutching her shoulder.

The big black cases loomed in front of her, taunting. They weren't locked. She could open them and examine the contents to try to figure out where they were going. She imagined sterile white walls and rows of hospital beds. No! She wouldn't jinx Kale by thinking of Ramstein.

Maybe they'd gotten word that he was coming home.

She shot to her feet, a burst of elation numbing her shoulder pain. They could be planning to meet him at the base, and they were going to tell her tonight at dinner. They'd probably leave early tomorrow morning. She swung around the glossy newel post to hurry back to her dinner preparations. If Kale's unit—

Her gaze landed on a colorful folio lying on the sideboard, and her thoughts screeched to a halt. Those were plane tickets. Amber rubbed her suddenly damp palms on her jeans. The constant tug of conflicting emotions made her stomach roll.

She shouldn't look at the tickets. She'd jumped to conclusions, thinking the trip had anything to do with Kale. They could be going on vacation after the holidays, even if Christmas was still a week away. Kale's mom always liked to prepare for travel early.

But not this early.

Amber's feet carried her closer to the oak sideboard. The folder screamed for attention, lying all alone next to simple silver candlesticks. If their cherubic nativity scene had been set up like it was supposed to be, Amber never would have spotted the piece of paper. Peeking inside would be a betrayal of the trust they'd bestowed when they gave her a key. But doing this, and hiding it from her—wasn't that a betrayal, too?

No, that wasn't fair. She wasn't their daughter, even if they'd filled in for her parents in some ways since the car crash that killed them nearly five years ago. The Rikers didn't owe her anything.

But they owed their son. And Amber was Kale's representative at home, wasn't she?

She twisted to see the clock over the fireplace. Five o'clock. They'd be on their way home from work, and never used the cell phone in the car. She couldn't wait. Her brain would drive her insane with all the possibilities. Her hand shook, but she reached for the packet and peeled back the corner, looking for the date of departure. *If it's after the New Year…*

The letters and numbers were stark black against the pale green ticket stock. December nineteenth. That was tomorrow. They were leaving tomorrow. She closed her eyes and swayed, catching herself against the heavy piece of furniture. Her heartbeat roared in her ears, the silence and staleness of the house pressing in around her.

A wave of cold air struck her. She turned to the open front door, where Kale's parents stood. His mother looked sad, his father grimly determined. Amber didn't give a second's thought to the fact that she'd been caught. All she could think was *what the fuck?*

"What is this?" Her voice came out high. She brandished the folder. "Where are you going?"

"We're taking a cruise." Arthur stood straight, defiant. "Two weeks in the Caribbean. Long overdue." He strode past her into the kitchen, his knee-replacement waddle more pronounced than usual. A moment later the silverware drawer rattled and cupboard doors banged.

"I don't understand." Amber swallowed back anger. "Why would you leave now?"

Dorothy pressed her lips together and stared up at Amber for a few seconds, her eyes watery. Amber was struck by how frail she was, her skin papery and loose. She'd always appeared old to Amber, because she and Arthur hadn't had Kale until they were in their mid-forties, but now the wrinkles seemed deeper, the circles under her eyes darker. She'd lost weight in the last few months. How had Amber missed it?

"I'm sorry, dear, I need to go lie down. The shop was busy today. Arthur can explain." She started slowly up the steps, her face turned resolutely away.

Amber set the plane tickets where she'd found them and braced herself to enter the kitchen. "Arthur?"

"You left the chicken out. It's contaminating the entire counter." He chucked the sweating package in the trash, ignoring Amber's cry of protest, and scrubbed at the counter with a soapy sponge.

She'd never seen him like this. "What's going on?"

He glanced at her, faded blue eyes snapping. "I told you. We're going to the Caribbean. For two weeks."

"But what if Kale comes home?"

"He's not coming home."

Amber flinched and felt her face flush. *Don't lash out.* Maybe she didn't know all the facts. "Did you hear something? Did he call?"

"No. That's the point. We haven't heard anything from anyone for half a year. It's been three months since they declared him missing. He's *not coming home.*"

Amber shook her head, afraid to look away from him, her heart breaking at the pain he must be feeling. "Of course he's coming home," she reassured him. "You have no reason to believe otherwise."

He just glowered at her as if she were stupid. Her flush

deepened, and this time she was unable to hold back the rush of anger. The argument she'd laid out in a relentless litany since Kale had been deployed rolled through her head. If he were dead, the military would have sent someone to the Rikers' house to notify them, released his body to the family if they could, and given him a hero's burial. They'd received no such notification. Nothing at all, in fact, for months.

Too many months.

Kale had contacted home whenever he could. The haphazard nature of the communication had been difficult, but Amber hadn't expected anything less. She'd done a lot of research in those first weeks, wanting to give them the best chance she could. Deployment statistics were bad enough for couples who had been married for years. She and Kale had only been together a few weeks before his deployment.

His leaves were short and infrequent, but they packed a lot into the time and reinforced the love they'd declared before he left. The last time she saw him, two Christmases ago, she'd faced the final stretch of his service with ease. It was almost over, and they could spend the rest of their lives together.

Then something changed.

At first, when she didn't hear anything from him for several weeks—all her e-mails going unanswered, her mail sent back unopened—she assumed he'd changed his mind about her. Maybe even met someone else. Eventually, she asked his parents if they'd talked to him. When they said they hadn't, the growing pain of rejection had chilled to fear. Was he missing in action? A prisoner? On an assignment that required him to go dark? None of the possibilities she dreamed up made complete sense, especially as time went on...and on. His parents inquired through channels and were told only that Kale would make contact as soon as he was able, and they were not at liberty to discuss the nature of his work.

That alone was difficult enough. Amber found herself stuck, unable to plan for the future, unwilling to act like there wouldn't be one. And then, three months ago, all the news outlets exploded over an unidentified squad of servicemen captured, killed on film, and buried in as-yet-undiscovered graves. The government denied any such thing had occurred, but within days the Rikers received notice that their son was missing in action, with no other details confirmed or conveyed "at this time." Amber seemed to be the only one who refused to connect the two.

Arthur rinsed the sponge and dropped it into its holder on the edge of the sink. "We're old, Amber. We can't endure this anymore. You know Dottie's been sick. It gets worse every day we don't get word, every holiday that he's not here."

"But we just need to have hope—"

"Hope means fear. And it's tearing her up inside." A strand of hair from his comb-over drooped, exposing his scalp and making him look uncomfortably vulnerable. He straightened and swept his hand over the top of his head. "It's tearing you up, too. You can't deny that."

She tossed up her hands. "What do you think I can do about it? I can't change what is."

"You can move on."

Her breath hitched. "What?" she managed to croak.

"Dottie won't get better if she doesn't start moving through the grieving process." The way he said it made it clear he meant himself too, but he was part of a generation that wouldn't discuss such things. "We just have to accept that our son—" His voice quavered. "Our son is gone." He pressed the side of his fist to his mouth. Amber wanted to put her arms around him but doubted he would accept that right now.

He cleared his throat and dropped his hand. "You should do the same."

"I can't." Images flashed behind her eyes. Some people worried about forgetting what someone had looked like when they were gone for a long time. Amber didn't have that problem. Moments in time were captured like GIFs. Kale grinning down at her, a towel around his neck, his hair sticking up all over the place. In his Santa suit, sitting on the throne-like wooden chair in the rec center, pulling her onto his lap and taking advantage of the very short skirt of her red-and-white Santa's helper costume. The night he told her he loved her, need burning so brightly in his eyes, burying the terror he refused to let her see.

Standing proud and tall and solemn in his uniform on deployment day, ready to fulfill his oath to his country.

He'd fulfill his oath to her, too.

"I believe in him," she whispered, then said it again, louder. "I believe in him."

Arthur shook his head. "I'm sorry, sweetheart." He glanced around the kitchen, as if extending the apology to everything he'd done and said in the last few minutes. Amber didn't care about trashed chicken, and no simple "sorry" could compensate for giving up.

She stood, teeth gritted and fists clenched, as he limped past her and out of the room. The stairs creaked under the pressure of his slow steps, and their weary weight eased the tension from her shoulders. She sighed and slumped into a gingham-cushioned kitchen chair. How could she be mad at them? They thought they'd lost their only son, the miracle baby that had given their lives meaning and purpose. Maybe the only way they could live was by accepting that he hadn't.

The pain in her chest throbbed. The Rikers' decision to proceed as if their son was gone wasn't the cause. It didn't shake Amber's conviction that Kale was alive and would be home soon. No, it was their dismissal of her that hurt so much.

She pushed to her feet and reached for the container of

mushrooms, placing them back in the grocery bag. Onions, butter, a box of pasta all followed. She stuffed the bouquet of chrysanthemums and alstroemeria for the centerpiece on top and strode back to the table to put on her down jacket.

They could have invited her to go with them on the cruise. Maybe it was too hard, living through another Christmas in Hempfield without Kale or any news of his return date. Maybe a cruise was a good idea. But they didn't have to abandon their son. Abandon her.

She stepped outside, making sure the door locked behind her, and sniffled into her mitten. It was full dark outside now, the sidewalks icy. A few cars passed on the crowded residential street, but people drove into their garages and avoided the frigid air.

She stared at the stars in the clear, cold sky, and wondered what they looked like to Kale. No, it wouldn't be night over there. Wherever "there" was. She wished she had some clue, some way to feel connected to him. She opened her eyes wide, watching for a shooting star to wish upon. A cloud drifted toward the slivered moon, and she zeroed in on it. *If the cloud covers the moon before the next car passes…*

A light honk pulled her attention from the sky, and she realized how freaking cold she was. She waved back at Colette, the high school teacher driving by, and hustled her stuff to the car. She didn't want to think about the Rikers or their belief of what happened to Kale, so on the drive home she ran down a mental list of the things she had to do over the next couple of days. The biggest job was helping set up the rec center for Christmas Eve, when Santa gave out presents to Hempfield's neediest kids and then hosted a big party for anyone who wanted to come. Kale used to play Santa, but their friend Danny had filled in for the last few years. There were donated presents to wrap and label, cookies to bake, and the Santa suit and helper costume to be picked up from the dry cleaners.

She had to work a shift at the soup kitchen, drop cleaned and sorted party clothes at the women's and children's shelter, and help put together three dozen Christmas dinner gift baskets to be delivered to families the morning before Christmas.

If Kale were here, she wouldn't have time to do any of that. When he got home, she'd have to shift a lot of her responsibilities to other people. Maybe she should start now. They were too reliant on her, and she didn't want to feel torn. Kale would deserve her full attention, and even if people understood why she was suddenly unavailable, it wouldn't stop them from needing her.

The next two weeks would be hard, with the Rikers gone and Amber having to face Christmas Eve and the site of some of her happiest memories alone. But not as hard as whatever Kale faced overseas. Now she had a plan, and that gave her strength. She would survive this, and so would Kale.

Chapter Two

The sun blazed out of a pale sky, bouncing off rocks and sand, radiating in every direction. Kale, prone between a boulder and a ragged rock face, hadn't moved in so long he thought his body might literally be cooked. The breeze that kicked up every so often did nothing more than blow sand in his face.

He blinked dust out of his eyes and repositioned the binoculars. His index finger nudged the focus button until his view into the shack's window was crisp.

Their mission target reportedly had a mole directly below the right corner of his mouth and a scar bisecting his left eyebrow. Both identifying marks were clear on the man centered in Kale's glasses. Thank God. He was so done with all of this. Done with the sand, the heat, the setbacks. Done with the shadow world he'd lived in for far too long.

Their last two missions had resulted in the capture of two warlords who had been terrorizing locals and the humanitarian groups trying to bring them food and medicine. Those successes had spoiled Kale and his team. They'd expected this mission to go the same way. Easy in, easy out, leaving this part of the world a marginally better place.

He should have known better. Completing this mission would get Kale home. So of course it was FUBAR from the get-go. Bad intel, malfunctioning equipment, a freaking flu sweeping through the team. You name it, it had bitten them in the ass.

But not this time.

So focus, asshole. They'd finally found the tangos they were tasked to bring in. Bad enough the predicted window meant they had to do this during the day. He had damned well better not fuck it up just because he could only think about Christmas and the plan he'd refined in his head over long hours of forced downtime.

He thumbed his throat mike. "Jacobus. Report." He listened to his team members repeat the details they'd laid out fifteen minutes ago. It was easy to concentrate during the reports, but once they all lapsed into silence again, his mind drifted back to the last time he saw Amber. Her flippy little red skirt revealing her gorgeous legs. Creamy cleavage flashing at him every time she set a baby on his knee. Her laughter, the love in her eyes, the way she went all serious when he pulled her down into his lap. Her warm mouth opening for him, her hands clutching the thick sleeves of his Santa suit, her throat releasing a quiet moan.

Fuck. He had to stop that. Distraction was a bigger enemy than the tangos in that shack. He was better than this.

He snorted at the irony. So much time had passed since that goodbye precisely because he was so good at his job. When he returned from his last leave, his commanding officer told him he'd been selected for a black ops mission that required him to go dark. He'd been excited, God help him. Chosen for a joint service team to infiltrate enemy territory and take out a heinous criminal most people back home didn't even know existed. They'd done so well on that first mission they were released to the jurisdiction of an alphabet soup of "security" agencies and assigned to one task after another. Then the team leader was wounded and sent home, and Kale was promoted. At first, he hadn't paid attention to how much time had passed, how long he'd gone without talking to Amber or his parents. He was that driven, that involved in their assignments. But then one of the guys mentioned his ex, and it flipped a switch in Kale's brain.

The shadow agency had selected him and the rest of the team because they were dedicated, skilled servicemen with no major outside obligations. But that was on paper. None of them were married or had kids, but that didn't mean they hadn't left anyone behind.

Too much time had passed. All of them had been here longer than they'd expected. Kale's original discharge was supposed to go through a year ago, but when he agreed to this transfer, he missed the part where it obligated him to additional time and nullified the letter he'd dropped to resign his commission. After fighting for months, he'd finally gotten them to agree to resubmit his letter so he could go home. *After* this mission was over.

His watch vibrated. Time to move. One last report to confirm the details. Four men, all armed, plus the leader. No civilians, children, women. They just needed to clear the way. Kale tasked his ordnance expert with scouting the open land between their hiding place on the bluff and the shack, laid out the plan, and set it in motion.

The stopwatch in his brain ticked off the time as they leapfrogged into position around the outside of the shack. The tangos' voices came through the open window, only so much babble to Kale. He pressed his comm deeper into his ear so Stelmat's translation was clearer. The targets were planning an attack on a nearby village, one friendly to the occupying forces. Exactly the reason Kale's team had been given to round up this group.

Kale gave the order to move in.

Bodies in motion, controlled, determined. Choreographed by thousands of hours of training and working together. Then shouts. Short bursts of fire. The tangos on the ground, secured. Stelmat slammed the leader against the wall, his hands already strapped. All according to plan.

Except the leader was…laughing.

Shit.

Kale shouted an order too late. A trapdoor burst open and two men came out firing before their heads even cleared the floor. Kale's men fired back, diving for cover. Everyone was shouting—his team, the tangos, their boss. Kale flipped the table over and braced his arms on its edge, taking careful aim with his sidearm. He fired. One shooter down. He squeezed the trigger again…and the world exploded in a wave of red with golden lights.

• • •

The world was muffled, wavery. Peaceful, until half a dozen bodies sank in bursts of bubbles around him. He pushed upward, his lungs burning. Shouts resolved into catcalls and laughter just before Kale blew up out of the frigid lake.

He noisily filled his lungs and hooted. "Holy hell, that's cold!"

"Serves you right, dude!" his friend Danny taunted from the dock. He shook a big fluffy towel. "We're waiting for you. It's all warm and cozy." He rubbed the terrycloth on his cheek.

Around Kale, Hempfield's bravest—or most stupid— gasped and spluttered or swept sheets of water at each other. Screw that. He was getting out! His limbs shook as he stroked the distance back to the dock. Why the hell had he jumped so far off the end? In the summer he'd have made the distance in ten seconds. Right now, every overhead pull took him half as far as it should.

He shuddered as hot hands helped him up the ladder, then let him go to assist the other noble idiots participating in the Polar Bear Plunge to benefit kids with cancer. Danny tossed the towel around his shoulders and pushed Kale down the dock where volunteers waited with hot cocoa, coffee, and clothes.

"Fleece first." Amber shoved a thick sweatshirt over Kale's head and helped him feed his hands through the sleeves. "Here." She stuck a cup of cocoa in his hand and knelt at his feet to hold the waistband of his sweatpants open. "Hurry. Your teeth are chattering."

Kale clenched them together but didn't lift his foot. He and Amber had been part of the same big gang of friends for years. He'd had his eye on her for months, ever since she graduated from college. He'd asked her out and she said yes, but the night before their first date, her parents had been killed in a car accident. He'd ended up being the friend with a shoulder to cry on, instead.

Kale understood. His parents were older, so he expected to lose them earlier than most people did, but not as young as Amber had. She'd coped by throwing herself into community service and using the insurance money to open a consignment shop downtown. Kale had done what he could to help, and because Amber never mentioned their canceled date, he never did, either.

Part of him was waiting for her to be ready, to give him a sign that it was okay to try again. Time was running out. His training started in two weeks, and it was unfair for him even to consider pushing forward with her.

But she looked up at him now, laughing, her face glowing in the thin January sunlight, and his heart twisted. Her grief, his military service, the stress of a long-distance relationship, none *of it mattered. She was made for him.*

Kale came to with a hard gasp that sent a spasm of pain through his torso. There was still shouting, but it had purpose and control now. Faces faded in and out over him.

"Hang on, Captain."

Kale realized he was on his back on something hard. Metal. Light flashed, and his head swam and dipped. No. Not his head—or not *just* his head. He registered the *thwap thwap thwap* that matched the flashes of light and shadow. He was in an evac helo. Injuries. There were injuries.

"How many?" he croaked, lifting his head and shoulders so he could sit up. Agony arrowed through his side. Holy *fuck* what was wrong with him? The world had gone red again. He blinked to clear it, struggled to focus on the report his XO was trying to give him.

"...casualties, but—"

Kale fisted his left hand around Jacobus's vest. "What casualties?"

"None for us, sir. We have two seriously wounded. Stelmat has a busted leg and a neck injury. He's strapped down and stable. Three with superficial wounds. And you, sir, have a good-sized hole in your side."

No wonder he couldn't sit up. At least his men were alive. "The target?"

"Dead. On board."

Good. Mission accomplished. Now he just had to get home to Amber by Christmas Eve. He tried to calculate how many days he had for debriefing and travel, but his brain suddenly relaxed. He glanced at his arm. Something had pinched it a few seconds ago. A clear tube stretched up from the crook of his elbow. Shit, they were...

He stepped out of darkness into the light on her front porch. Amber smiled over her shoulder, one hand unlocking the deadbolt, the other twisting the doorknob. Kale was afraid to interpret that smile. Yeah, this had been their best date yet. Not just dinner and a movie but a long walk around the lake, lots of heated kisses, even deep discussion about hopes and dreams and the future. All the things women dug and men usually dreaded. But Kale had loved every minute of it.

He was so fucking gone over this woman.

But would she invite him in? He was leaving tomorrow and had no right to ask her to wait for him. Not after a two-week—was he really thinking of it this way?—courtship.

But she grabbed him by the tie and jerked him after her into the dark living room. The door slammed behind him and he followed it, surprised by the wildcat who shoved him backward and pressed herself full-body against him.

Kale recovered quickly. She smelled so damned good, fresh air and sweetness and desire. Her mouth tasted even better.

She laughed into the kiss. "Sleep with me now, for tomorrow you may die," she teased.

Kale didn't feel like laughing. He rested his forehead against Amber's and cuddled her close. His hands roamed up and down her back. "Don't joke."

She must have heard something in his tone. "I'm sorry." She caressed his face. "Are you afraid?"

Of dying? No. Of being away from her, of losing her—hell, yes. He was even more afraid of expressing it after they'd been together such a short time.

Okay, expressing it again. He couldn't believe he'd blurted it out like that. It was just that she'd been so beautiful, so full of life and laughter. So much of everything he wanted to protect, a symbol of all his reasons for joining the military. He wanted her to know, before he abandoned her, how much she meant to him.

Back at the lake she'd only hugged him hard, then kissed him with hunger that had pulled them back here for privacy. Kale had warred with himself the entire walk. His noble side *was losing badly before they even reached her walkway. Now it lay broken and battered next to the lustful winner.*

"I really do love you," he whispered. "I hate myself for even telling you that. But I wanted you to know before I leave. I'm not just trying to get my rocks off while I still can."

She laughed and rubbed her body against his. "I know that. And I have a secret." She backed up, her hands hooked into his jacket, pulling him with her. She never looked behind her, but dragged him up the stairs and down the hall to her bedroom.

"What's your secret?" Kale could hardly breathe—exactly how he'd been when he came out of the lake and found Amber kneeling at his feet. She sank to her knees again and reached for his belt buckle.

"I love you, too." And she proceeded to take him to heaven.

Kale's brain went fuzzy. The darkness in the room faded into light. He struggled to hold on, but consciousness slowly overtook him.

He opened his eyes. Pale walls, limp curtains around his bed, an IV pole on his left, and beeping equipment on his right. Hospital sounds filtered from beyond the curtains, nothing frantic or hurried, just day-to-day business.

He lay there for a few minutes, absorbing. Letting the dream-memory fade so he could concentrate on reality. He had to get up. Find out his men's status. What day it was. How fucked up *he* was.

He pulled the monitoring clip off his finger and the EKG pads off his chest—wincing at the hair they took with them—and tried to roll to his left. Pain blazed as badly as it had before, deep into his right side. He blistered the air with curses and forced himself upright. With his hand clamped over the bandages on his side, he breathed through the pain.

He sat hunched until it subsided and his vision cleared. He reached for support, and his hand found the IV pole. It was cold against his palm as he dragged himself to his feet.

Sweat popped out on his forehead and neck, and the floor threatened to smack him in the face.

"Oh, no you don't!" A nurse whipped back the curtain and braced strong hands on his shoulders.

"I need to—"

"Get updates on your team. I know the drill." Somehow, she maneuvered him back onto the bed against his will, releasing him to work the bed's controls. The top half rose to meet him, and Kale tried to hide his relief at the support. She smirked and adjusted the blankets over his legs. "You guys are all the same, and every one of you thinks you can get past me." She charged on, her rant convincing Kale he wasn't going to succeed where seemingly everyone before him had failed.

When she wound down, he asked, "What day is it?"

"December twentieth." She checked the contents of a pitcher on the little table next to the bed. "You need ice. I'll get that and the OIC to come answer your questions. Don't move."

Kale found himself smiling. Nurses had it all over officers as far as giving orders. But the amusement faded when no one came to brief him. What had happened during his lost hours? He didn't remember anything after the sedative on the helicopter. He'd give Jacobus hell for that, if he didn't know it had probably been necessary. For damned sure, if they hadn't knocked him out, he'd have tried to get up to take over the situation. That was his job.

Or it had been. He hoped to hell his job was over. If he remembered right, Jacobus had told him the target was killed in the firefight. They'd been ordered to capture him, so the mission wouldn't be considered successful. But it would be marked complete, and that was all Kale needed to get out.

Hopefully they would debrief him and wrap up the details in time for him to go home. He could still make it by Christmas Eve.

A few months ago, after he'd bought the engagement ring that hadn't left his body since, he and the guys had been hanging around watching one of the random DVDs people sent in care packages from the States. They'd ripped into the ridiculous surprise-reunion-at-Christmas storyline, but it had gotten Kale thinking. Women loved that shit, and public homecomings were almost bigger Internet porn than LOLcats. His go-to memory was playing Santa, with Amber as his helper, on their last Christmas Eve together. It was the perfect time to propose. Four days was cutting it close, but if he pushed—

"Captain Riker." A tall balding man pushed aside the dangling curtain between beds and stepped into Kale's cubicle. He wore a silver eagle and a nametag that said "DiPaolo." The nurse closed the curtain behind him. Her shoes squeaked softly as she left them alone.

"Sir."

"This is not a secure ward." DiPaolo glanced around then pulled a rolling stool under his ass, wheeling as close to Kale as he could. "I don't have the authority to give you a full debriefing or report here. But I think if we keep you in the dark more than a few minutes, you'll be tearing down the walls looking for answers."

"Yes, sir." Kale curbed his frustration. "I was told some of my men were badly hurt."

"Stelmat has a broken leg with some torn tendons and sufficient damage to be sent home for rehabilitation. His neck injury was not as major as feared in the field. Three of your team were treated on base with minor injuries and are pending reassignment."

Kale nodded to acknowledge the report, but had to hide his dismay. He wanted to be done, yes, but this wasn't how he wanted his team to break up. He had no idea what reassignment would mean in the shadows. If they stayed dark, he wouldn't be allowed to contact them from the outside.

"Your situation is more serious," DiPaolo continued. "I'm told they expect to move you to a semi-private room today. Now that you're awake, your condition will likely be upgraded from critical but stable to recovering. We've tried to contact your parents, but have been unable to reach anyone."

He should call them. He didn't want a stranger telling them he was hurt, and they could help him with the surprise. "I'd like to call them myself, sir, when we're done here."

But DiPaolo shook his head. "We're in a communications blackout, probably until Tuesday."

Fuck. That meant there'd been an incident, and they were making the worst kind of notifications. He wouldn't be allowed to log in to freaking Facebook until the blackout was lifted. No matter. He'd be home by then.

"How soon can I leave?" he asked.

"That's yet to be determined. A couple of weeks, at least."

"No." Kale pushed himself higher on the pillows and tried not to reveal the new wave of agony weakening his muscles. "I need to be home for Christmas. Christmas Eve. I know we can't complete my termination that fast, but I was promised—"

"I know what you were promised."

Kale frowned at DiPaolo's tone. Was he going to block him?

He chose his words carefully. "I hope there's no problem with that promise, sir."

"The problem isn't with your termination, Riker, but with your condition. There's no way they're letting you out of here in the next two days."

Chapter Three

"**B**ingo!"

The activities room of the Holly Glen Home for Active Living buzzed with the disappointment of a few dozen senior citizens and their guests. Amber stared in mock dismay at her nearly full card. "No way, Rose! I only needed two more!"

Rose cackled and accepted her prize, a super-soft plush rabbit, from the teenager who carried it over. Her gnarled hands shook as she turned the bunny to face her, and a deep sigh ended the cackle. "This is just like the one Caitlyn sleeps with every night."

Amber doubted Rose's granddaughter still slept with stuffed animals. The girl was nineteen, a freshman in college. But her family had moved to Colorado years ago and rarely came home to visit. It broke Rose's heart that her only grandchild had chosen a college even farther away, in Oregon.

The runner bent and kissed Rose on the cheek. "I brought that one 'specially for you, Ms. Rose. Congratulations on winning."

Rose smiled and patted her hand. The girl went back to the snack table, and Rose caught Amber watching the interaction with, she was sure, way too much sympathy on her face. The old woman's expression went soft and shrewd at the same time.

"Sometimes we just need to let them go, don't we?" She tucked the rabbit next to her in her wheelchair and ran a magnetic wand over her metal-ringed playing pieces to collect them.

Amber, who didn't have fancy bingo gear, crumpled her marked-up paper and tore a new one off the pad in the center of the table. "Let what go? Teenagers? In some ways, yes."

"Not just teenagers," Rose scoffed. "Everyone who's no longer in our lives. At some point, we have to just accept that they're gone." She wheezed a little and paused to catch her breath.

Amber tried to keep her expression clear and reached for a pitcher to pour Rose some water. "I suppose, when it's impossible for someone to come back, it's healthier to move on. For our own well-being. But Rose," she continued before the woman could make her point more bluntly. "Caitlyn isn't gone. She's just far away. You'll see her soon."

"Everybody ready for the next round?" Chad, the Holly's activities director, vigorously rotated the drum of bingo balls. A few shouts of "ready!" rose above the clatter.

Rose scooped up a pile of chips in one hand. "Maybe. I'll ship her presents anyway. Better than leaving them lying around forever."

Amber snorted at the not-so-subtle jab. Apparently, it was common knowledge that she had a stockpile of presents for Kale from birthdays, holidays, and anniversaries he hadn't been home for. This afternoon, Amber had taken Rose for some last-minute shopping downtown. While Rose debated between pairs of gloves for her beau, Amber had come across a leather excursion messenger bag. Kale used to talk about the business he intended to start when he got out. The bag was expensive, and Rose hadn't withheld her opinion of "wasteful spending on things no one would ever get to use."

"O-62," Chad called. "That's O. Sixty. Two."

Amber X-ed through the space with a pencil and studied her game cards. Between them, she had the numbers relating to her birthday, Kale's birthday, the day he said he loved her, and the day he was deployed. *If all of those numbers get called…*

"B-1. B. One."

None of the cards on Amber's strip had that one. Rose snapped two markers down.

"The point is," she said, scouring the half-dozen cards in front of her, "sometimes people won't be back. Sometimes they can't be. And the way of the world is that not everything gives us a solid finish." Satisfied that she didn't have any other squares to mark, Rose raised her head. "Do I need to spell it out for you, dear?"

Amber forced herself to laugh even though she'd rather snap at her. "He's not dead, Rose. I won't believe it. I can't. That choice is doing much more good than harm, trust me."

Something caught Rose's attention behind Amber, and her wrinkles rearranged themselves into that crafty expression women of her age had perfected when they decided to become matchmakers. "*Some* people would beg to differ."

Amber didn't have to look to know who had walked into the room. The other night, after the shock at the Rikers' house, she'd called her cousin Rina for commiseration. Rina had been Amber's best friend for two and a half decades and formed her one-woman family support team since Kale left. But she'd almost seemed to be on the Rikers' side when she said Danny, a guy Amber had known since kindergarten, was waiting for her as patiently as she'd been waiting for Kale.

Danny owned the hardware store next to Amber's consignment shop. They saw each other every day, shared coffee, took turns bringing each other lunch, and volunteered on a few of the same committees. Rina thought Danny did some of those things for other reasons, not because he liked to do them. But he knew as well as anyone that Amber's heart belonged to Kale.

Okay, not *everyone* seemed convinced. Rose made eyes at Amber, then at whoever approached behind her.

"Hello, beautiful." Danny braced his hand on the back of Amber's chair to bend and give Rose a hug. "You win yet?"

"Of course." She showed him her rabbit.

Danny's big hands stroked over the soft fur. Amber sat back in her chair, tuning out Danny's rumbling voice as he chatted with Rose. He was an attractive guy. His strong, capable hands were connected to powerful arms and a gracefully carved torso. Quick to smile, quicker to laugh, Danny was more compassionate than half the people Amber knew who pretended to be do-gooders because it elevated their own social standing. He was a great guy, and he deserved a great woman.

Someone who wasn't her.

He examined her bingo cards. "Aren't you paying attention? He called three numbers." He picked up her pencil and quickly marked off the ones she'd missed.

"Thanks. Just thinking."

He circled behind her to claim an empty chair and ripped off a playing strip for himself. "Let's see if I can catch up here."

Rose cast proud glances between the two of them for the rest of the session, but despite her split attention, she still managed to win two more times.

After the games were over, Amber helped clean up and then made the rounds to say goodbye to Rose and the rest of her friends at the Holly. By the time she left, it had gotten dark outside, and colder than the night before. She zipped her parka all the way up and paused on the building's front porch to pull on her gloves. Her breath misted in front of her, pale in the glow from the overhead lamp. The street was quiet, with most guests exiting to the rear parking lot. After the excess heat and noise of the activities room, Amber savored the silence and chill.

Her thoughts drifted again to the pile of gifts under the Christmas tree at home. Some had football wrapping paper, some pumpkin. One, her favorite, wasn't wrapped. It commemorated the day Kale told her he loved her. They'd been walking around the lake after a dinner date. It had been warmer than it was now, and the park's pair of swans was out. They did the thing where they curved their necks and touched beaks so they looked like a heart. Kale had just blurted it out—*I love you*—no preliminaries, no warning. Amber, already on an emotional precipice, had tumbled hard. Since then, swans had been her touchstone, symbolized by a necklace from Kale that she never took off. Last year at a yard sale, she found a ridiculous-looking stuffed swan dressed in battle fatigues and bought it for a dollar. Kale would have found it hilarious.

Would have…

The cold air crystallized in her lungs. She hadn't just thought that. He *will* find it hilarious, she corrected furiously. She would not let the people in this town, with all their well-meant fatalism, weaken her convictions.

And she would not burst into tears standing here alone in the dark. She glanced down to gauge the distance to the first step, but before she lifted a foot, a voice hit her out of the darkness, making her jump.

"Heading home?"

She whipped around to see Danny leaning against the first turn of the handicapped ramp. He'd been there a while, judging by his crossed feet and hands shoved deep in his pockets.

"You jerk." Amber tried to laugh, but it sounded like she was hacking up a hairball. "I didn't see you there."

"I know. Sorry." He pushed away from the rail and crossed the porch to her. "If you don't have your car, I'll walk you home."

"Thanks."

They passed the first block in silence. Danny seemed fine with it, but Amber couldn't ignore the opportunity to confront him. He'd been everywhere the last few days. At first she thought he was just being supportive at a time he knew was hard for her. But after Rina and now Rose had both indicated his feelings were stronger than that, Amber had to bring it out into the open.

"Kale is coming home," she said.

"I know." He sounded perfectly calm and comfortable with the idea.

"I love him."

"I know that, too." He took a longer stride to check the cross street, then let her catch up to him after he signaled the coast was clear. "But is the guy you love the one who's going to come home?"

She didn't have to ask what he meant. "Of course he won't be. I can't even imagine what kinds of horrors he's seen, what he's done." What had been done to him. She shoved away the thought. "But I don't care. He's mine."

Danny nodded as if he agreed. "What if you're not his?"

Wow. That was blunt. And Amber had no argument. Kale being dead was a possibility she had little trouble dismissing. Kale not wanting her anymore? That was a fear so big it didn't even fit in her brain.

When she didn't answer, Danny didn't press her. He let the question bounce around in her skull for another block.

They turned left onto Main Street. Cars zoomed past, and a few people hustled in and out of the stores, movie theater, and restaurants that made up downtown.

"I know the holidays are hard for you." Danny tilted his head back and squinted at an angel perched on a streetlight. "Has it gotten better or worse this year?"

"I don't know." Amber scuffed her foot. "I guess a little worse, with his parents preferring to think he's dead."

"Whoa." Danny stared down at her. "That's the first time I ever heard you say anything negative about them."

Amber shrugged. She'd tried hard not to resent them but was losing the battle. Every time someone gave her a sympathetic look or mentioned grieving or, like Rose, letting go, she knew it was because they were following the Rikers' lead.

They turned again, onto her street with its little brick Cape Cod houses, half of them surrounded by chain link fences to keep the dogs in. She'd left the light on next to the front door, and it beckoned to her. There was warmth in that house, and coziness. And incredible loneliness.

"Amber." Danny stopped her halfway up the walk to her steps. "Look at me."

She did, reluctantly, because if he didn't say what she expected him to, she'd have be the one to address it. The last thing she wanted was to hurt him or anyone else.

He settled his hands on her shoulders and stared down into her eyes. His were gray-blue where Kale's were bright blue, but they held affection, hope, concern, and maybe even love. He hadn't worn a hat on his light brown hair—again, different from Kale's short, dark waves.

Before she'd even finished the comparison, Danny had tugged her closer, bent, and laid his mouth over hers.

Cold immediately turned to warmth. Amber hadn't been kissed in three years, and part of her clung to the simple joy of human touch. But that was all she felt. There was no cascade of goosebumps when his tongue stroked her lips. No burn of desire down deep, or craving to be closer, to have more of him. He smelled good, and they were obviously compatible. But Amber knew if ever she allowed a relationship between them, it would be comfortable and sweet and nothing like what she knew she and Kale would have.

Amber took one step back, breaking the circle of his arms. He let them fall. The cold rushed between them, and Danny didn't speak but was clearly waiting to hear her reaction.

"Everyone keeps telling me to move on." She cleared her throat. "They point out that if I did, you'd be there, waiting."

"I am." His expression was still hopeful, but held a new reserve that made Amber's heart ache. She didn't want to hurt him, but it would be better to do it now, definitively, than to let him keep hoping when there was no reason to.

She had to take a moment to fight a sense of futility that had nothing to do with Danny. *No notification, no body, no twenty-one-gun salute*, she reminded herself.

"You can't," she said simply, and he nodded. But what he said wasn't what she expected.

"Your loneliness kills me."

Amber's eyes stung with sudden tears. She hadn't even noticed how lonely she really was until a few minutes ago—or hadn't been honest with herself about it—and it had clearly been obvious to Danny all along.

She still tried to deny it. "I have a very rich life full of friends."

"I know. But none of them gives you what Kale did, and you deserve it. Love, a partner, a family. I can do that, Amber." He held up a hand. "I know you're not ready to consider it. I just wanted you to know that I *am* here. I care about you more than you realize. And I didn't want you to dismiss us as a possibility."

Because she was pining for a dead man. That was what he meant.

"Is that why you kissed me?" She sniffed and swept her glove across her cheek. "To make me think about possibilities?"

He nodded. "Did it work?"

There was only one thing to say. "I'm sorry," she whispered. "No."

After Danny gave her a sad, resigned goodbye kiss on the cheek, after Amber wrapped Kale's new leather bag and put it under the tree for him, she lay alone in her bed, in the dark, and wondered.

Had Kale's kisses really made her feel so very different from Danny's? Or was that just how she *remembered* they felt? Maybe her memories weren't real. Maybe she'd enhanced them over time. Maybe, even if they were real, Kale didn't share her feelings.

What if his had faded while she'd turned hers into some impossible ideal he could never live up to?

Was holding on to him noble and loyal? Or foolish and cowardly because she didn't want to risk getting hurt again?

Chapter Four

Fever dreams, they were called. And they sucked ass. Unlike the dream-memories of his best Amber moments, these were full of anxiety and desperation. Worse, they made it impossible to convince the doctors he was well enough to be shipped stateside.

He did everything the nurses told him to, despite the instincts that urged him to get out of bed and run a few miles to prove he was fine. He took his antibiotics, drank gallons of whatever they gave him, forced down food he had no appetite for—every bite making him miss Amber's cooking even more—and slept as much he could.

And dreamed.

His father loved to tell stories. "Frank was so mad at the guy just standing around, he asked how much he made a week. The guy said about three hundred dollars, so Frank peeled that out of his money clip, shoved it in his hand, and said, 'take it, and you're fired!' When he asked the supervisor how long he'd been working there, the guy told him he didn't! He was just delivering a pizza!"

Everyone howled with laughter. Kale grinned at his mother's indulgent head-shake and the tears Amber had to wipe from her eyes. "We should make this a tradition," he said, feeling stupidly sentimental. "No matter what's going on for the holidays, exactly one week before, we should all have dinner. Amber's chicken marsala." He forked a bite as everyone agreed, but then his father began another story, and everyone ignored Kale.

His father's voice began to warble like a bad radio. The table stretched and stretched until Amber and his parents were at the other end, talking avidly, leaving Kale by himself at the far end of the room.

"Hey!" he called, testing. "Someone pass the salt!" No one moved. They didn't seem to hear him. He pushed his chair back and stood. That worked, but when he tried to walk along the side of the table, tried to reach for Amber, nothing happened. He couldn't touch her. Couldn't make progress on the slick floor. The harder he tried, the more he hurt. Burning in his side. He looked down. His fatigues were red with blood.

"Time for meds!" a cheery voice rang into the dream, and Kale blinked his eyes open. Thank God. That wasn't how that night had gone at all. His father's stories, yeah, but Kale had sat next to Amber instead of at the end of the table. Their thighs had pressed together, and Amber kept giving him little touches. Stroking his hair from his temple to the back of his neck. Gripping his arm when she laughed or remembered something. They'd made the meal together, the two of them, and Kale had been struck by the rightness of everything. He'd wanted to propose to Amber right then, but he still had just under a year to go before he could leave active duty. So he'd suggested the tradition, instead. They'd all loved the idea.

And then he'd fucked things up. They'd have had that meal a couple of nights ago, without him. Again.

"Come on," the nurse urged, shaking the little paper cup

at him. "Last dose today. I think you're doing better."

Kale tossed the pills back and accepted the water she held for him. "Good enough to get out of here?"

She made a skeptical face. In a weak moment yesterday, he'd shown her the simple blue diamond he'd bought in Japan and carried through all his missions since. She'd been sympathetic, had given him a little extra attention to help him battle the infection, but she also kept telling him to manage his expectations.

"We'll see how you are tomorrow." She patted him on the shoulder and flipped off the light on the wall behind him. "Night, Captain."

"Night."

The sedative that was part of his nighttime dosage took effect quickly, pulling him down, down into dark nothingness. Next thing he knew he was standing in bright sunlight.

He hadn't seen Amber in weeks, and he ached at the sight of her running across the grass toward him. She slammed into his body, his arms wrapping around her and lifting her off the ground. He tasted salt, her tears cool on his cheek, but the kiss was hot and hungry. A command shouted by another officer interrupted the kiss. Kale stood with his unit, his parents, and Amber on the other side of the parking lot. Hundreds of duffel bags were lined up next to the curb. Soldiers' names were called and responded to.

"Riker."

He didn't want to go. But then he was inside the building, his backpack over one shoulder, surrounded by the men and women who had become his new family. Then outside again, standing alone while people wept and murmured and shouted around him. He had to find Amber, say his final goodbye, assure her they could get through this. He'd be in contact as often as he could. They'd write, they'd plan their future. Spend every leave together. He had to find her. Tell her he loved her.

Make sure she knew. Make sure she'd wait for him.
    She had to wait for him.

Kale looked out the window when he woke again, checking the position of the sun before he looked at the clock. Hard to tell from here, but he'd slept a lot today, so it had to be afternoon. Yeah, after three. He needed to talk to the doctor before he was gone for the day.

First, though, he took inventory. He maneuvered his hand around IV tubes and monitoring lines to lay his palm on his forehead. Dry. And miracle of miracles, cool. His mouth was a little gummy, but his throat wasn't stuck to itself like it usually was when he woke up in here. He bet his breath was deadly, but that didn't matter now. His stomach rumbled, and Kale smiled. Hunger. First time he'd wanted food since he got here.

Now for the real test. He fumbled for the bed controls and held his breath while he raised the head of the bed into a full sitting position. His side twinged, but he didn't have the burning, gut-deep pain from before. He forced himself to keep breathing while he tossed off the blanket and swiveled, much more carefully than the first time. When he pushed to stand, everything stayed right where it was supposed be.

Oh, yeah. He was getting out of here. Now he just had to convince the doctor and the OIC.

Two days before Christmas, and Amber couldn't figure out what to do with herself.

Tonight, miracle of miracles, no one needed her. Everything on her to do list was done, and she was free until it was time to put on her red velvet Santa's helper costume and hand out presents. But the emptiness of her house made her all too aware of the space inside her, so she dragged Rina out to Murphy's, the downtown pub, hoping the company

Christmas parties and celebrating singles would distract her. At minimum, it was an acceptable place to drink herself stupid.

"You're a great friend," she told her cousin, who had endured dozens of whinefests over their decades-long friendship. "Thanks for coming along and not being all psychologic-y and stuff." She pulled some of her frozen Brandy Alexander—her third—through a straw. Kirby, Murphy's bartender, really knew how to make the best drinks, especially the kind that let you get drunk without trying.

"Don't thank me yet. It's early." Rina twisted in her tall chair to survey the crowd. "You see any out-of-towners? I don't want to waste this dress."

"It's a good dress," Amber agreed. The plunging, overlapping neckline of brilliant blue silk showed off Rina's assets without looking trashy. Rina slung a long, smooth leg over the other knee and let her matching stiletto hang off her toes. "You have sexy-approachable down pat. Wish I could do that," she grumbled.

"No, you don't." Rina smiled at a guy at the bar, but then sighed and turned back to the small round table. "Damn, that's Fireman Fred."

"So?" Amber tried to squint past a group of women from the software company up the street.

"Been there, yada yada." Rina pulled a mozzarella stick from their basket and bit off a chunk. "He's okay in bed, but too eager. Needs a lot of encouragement. I'm too tired for that."

Amber had forgotten who they were talking about. Oh, yeah. Fireman Fred, assistant chief of the west side fire company. He bought jeans from her sometimes.

Rina checked her watch and leaned her head on her hand, elbow on the glossy table. "Look, I know you said you don't want psychologic-y stuff, but you know you have to talk about this, right?"

Amber stirred her drink with her straw, watching the air bubbles in the slush slide into different patterns. "Talk about what? It's the same old stuff as every year."

"No, it's not." Rina met Amber's gaze, and her eyes were kind, sympathetic.

Crap. "You talked to Danny, didn't you?" She didn't wait for Rina's nod. "I'm not talking about that."

"Okay."

Some of the tension inside Amber eased when Rina didn't push her. She shoved her straw deep into the curvy glass and sucked hard. The sharp, creamy cold hit her tongue and eased down her throat. "He deserves more than to be second best. He deserves someone to love him like I lo—" She stopped, infuriated by her inability to choose a verb tense.

"Like you love Kale," Rina said easily. "Or are you starting to question that?"

"Absolutely not."

"Okay then." Rina shrugged. "But somehow I don't think that's why we're at Murphy's tonight."

Amber looked miserably around the bar. Murphy's was more than a place to drink and hook up. It had the best comfort food in Hempfield, and everyone came here. "I can see at least four people who told me this week that I should give up on Kale and move on with my life."

Rina shrugged again and ate the rest of her cheese stick. "Moving on doesn't have to mean with Danny." She chewed slowly, savoring, and swallowed. "It could just mean to stop waiting." Her casually bored air disappeared and she studied Amber. "You've been in a holding pattern for a long time, now that I think about it."

"I don't know what you're talking about." Amber drank until her glass was exactly half-empty. Her head had gone swimmy, a nice change from the hard, intense circle of thoughts she couldn't escape. *If I can finish it before anyone else gives me advice…*

"Of course you do."

A tall, lanky guy in a trucker cap and red-and-green flannel button-down took a few steps in their direction.

Rina turned her back. His shoulders drooped. He sighed, shoved his hands in his pockets, and continued on to the bar. Amber hid her smirk in her melty brandy cream.

"What were you going to do with your degree when you graduated from college?" Rina asked her.

Amber frowned. Her degree was in merchandising with a minor in business. She'd interviewed at a couple of small chains and one major independent store in various cities, but had no job offers before her parents were killed and she had to come home. "I hadn't decided. But what does that have to do with Kale? We weren't together then."

"I know. But that's actually when you went into the holding pattern, wasn't it?"

"No. I just changed my goals, that's all."

Rina straightened, her eyes glinting. "Yeah. Changed from long-term, big-world goals to small-town, get-what-I-can-get goals. Right?"

Amber wanted to deny it, but Rina had her. "Okay, yeah. But it doesn't matter. I'm happy here. I have tons of friends, people I care about, who I've known all my life. If I can't have true family, that's the next best thing."

"But what do you also want that you can't have here? And don't say Kale."

She hadn't been about to. But she was a little stunned that the answer came so easily. Rina gave her a knowing smile when she didn't voice it, and she knew she didn't have to. She just needed to know it.

This wasn't the life she'd be living if things were different. Her shop was fine. It made her enough money to live on, since her parents' house was paid for and the cost of living here was reasonable. But it wasn't a challenge anymore. Planning, launching, and running a business had been great, but there was nowhere else to take it.

If she accepted the common belief that Kale was dead, what would she do with her life? Not her romantic life, but her *life* life?

She wouldn't stay in Hempfield.

It didn't free her. There was no miraculous lifting of weight or swelling of hope, because she *didn't* accept the common belief. Okay, yes, her resolve had been battered by the negative viewpoints of everyone around her. Their certainty that Kale was gone made her question whether she was being stupid, putting so much faith in something so unlikely.

But this wasn't *their* lives. It was hers, and what Rina just made her consider was likely to make life after Kale's return easier, not harder. With the clarity of the nearly drunk, she found that central core of faith and clutched it with both hands.

"Have I told you how much I love you?" she asked Rina, who grinned.

"You going mushy on me now?"

Amber shook her head. "No. I just really, really, *really* appreesheeate you." She scowled. That word had sounded funny. She peered into her empty glass. Whoa. That went fast. She blinked up at the twinkly lights around the perimeter of the bar. They hadn't been twinkly when they came in. "I think I shhhould probly eat shomething."

Rina pushed the appetizer a few inches toward her. "Have at it. But isn't getting sloppy in the head the reason we're here?"

Amber nodded and tried a cheese stick, grimacing at the rubbery texture. They were too cold, but the bite hit her stomach and suddenly she was ravenous. She signaled the server and ordered a cheeseburger and side salad. And a glass of water, to head off tomorrow's hangover.

"So what are you thinking now?" Rina asked. "About Kale."

"I don't know." Amber sighed and suppressed a burp. She hoped the kitchen was quick with that burger. "I guess we'll shee tomorrow night." Her words were still shlurry, and she had the vague sense that her thoughts were, too. But who cared? She felt better than she had yesterday. Better than today, when the mail carrier hung out in her store for ten minutes. He'd gone on and on about all the guys he knew who'd been messed up in the Iraqi and Afghan wars and hinted how much better off she was that Kale hadn't come back.

Who knew how she'd feel tomorrow? Especially when they did the Santa thing with the kids. She could get overwhelmed again. Despair was relentless, really. Wasn't that why Kale's parents had given in? Just like the townspeople. Amber knew they cared about her. That was why they were pushing her so hard. They wanted her to be happy. Or…no, that wasn't right. How could she be happy if she thought Kale was dead? So they wanted her to accept that he was dead because it was…healthier?

She narrowed her eyes at LaDonna, the flower and gift shop owner from across the street. She and her husband had passed Amber and Rina when they arrived. LaDonna had patted Amber sympathetically on the arm and told her she'd talked to Kale's mother a couple of days ago, and how sorry she was about his death. She'd clutched her husband's arm pretty damned tightly when she said it.

"Is that why they're ganging up on me?" she said aloud, snapping her back straight and almost toppling off the stool. She caught herself and held up a reassuring hand. "I'm good, I'm good. But seriously, is that why? Because they're trying to hide their own fears and securities?"

Rina laughed. "I think you mean insecurities, and I have no idea what train that thought traveled in on. But here's your food. We can debate small-town philosophies tomorrow."

Amber sprinkled salt on the cheesy patty and dug in. She probably nodded at Rina, because her cousin turned her attention to the trucker cap guy she'd blown off earlier and spelled something in the air with her finger.

Tomorrow might be worse, if she was hungover and depressed and the Relentless Relentertons kept on her. If Kale's parents called from their cruise and sounded at peace despite deciding to grieve their only son. If that meant Amber was even more alone in the world than she thought she was. And it might be worse if tomorrow was the day the U.S. Government came clean about what they'd done to one of their best men. Or if Kale finally showed his face and it was full of regret and "I'm sorry but I found someone I like better."

But tomorrow wasn't here yet.

Chapter Five

Kale stared at the seemingly endless flight of aluminum steps leading to the fourth and smallest airplane he'd been on in the last twenty-four hours, and had the thought that it was always the simple things that were hardest to overcome.

He'd convinced the doctor to release him to finish his recovery at home, and negotiated with DiPaolo to allow him to handle his own travel arrangements instead of waiting for a medical transport that wasn't scheduled for three more days.

It had started off fine. He'd heeded all the instructions to take it easy and used care getting on and off of two military transports and onto a major commercial flight. The problem came when that plane was grounded right before takeoff, and he'd had to rush all the way across the massive airport to his new plane. Running with the wound he had wasn't smart in the first place, and dodging an oblivious toddler had been his final downfall. He'd tripped over someone's carry-on, knocked into a recharging station, and gone down on one knee to avoid kicking an old lady's walker out from under her.

He'd made the flight but spent half of it in the bathroom, trying to stop the blood that kept oozing out of his side.

Now he stood on the tarmac outside some rinky-dink municipal airport somewhere in the States. He couldn't remember where he was. In the South, probably, since there was no snow and he was sweating his ass off. He had a vague awareness that it was mid-morning on Christmas Eve, with a three-hour flight to Boston and then a way-too-long drive to Hempfield still ahead of him. And he couldn't even manage to get up a couple dozen steps.

"Can I take that for you, sir?" A flight attendant in a snug blue skirt put her hand on his rucksack. Kale tightened his grip on the strap. He hadn't relinquished it to anyone the whole trip.

"No, thank you. I'm fine." He braced his legs to keep from swaying backwards and proving himself a liar. The attendant smiled and reached for the ticket in his hand. Kale took a deep breath and grabbed the aluminum rail. The hot sun reflecting off it seared both his eyes and his hand, but he ignored the insignificant pain and let the attendant slide his ticket between the fingers folded over his bag's strap.

"Your seat is in the rear of the plane, sir, right side, window."

Of course it was. "Thank you." Kale gritted his teeth and lifted his right leg. Salty sweat stung his eyes, but the real battle was fighting the hot poker stuck in his side. The left boot was easier. He pulled it up from the ground to the next step and pushed his weight upward. There. One down. All he needed was a rhythm. The attendant's sympathy and concern saturated the air even more than the humidity did. Kale ignored it. When it turned to impatience halfway up the steps, he ignored that too. Eventually he made the doorway and unclenched his jaw to breathe in the blissfully cool air in the plane's cabin.

The flight was packed. He stared at the empty seat waiting for him in the rear, but a sinking dread filled him the closer he got. That space wasn't even big enough for his left nut. How the hell was he going to cram himself into it in this condition? He'd be lucky if he didn't pass out before he sat down.

"Excuse, me, sir?"

A different attendant placed her hand on his arm. He turned and tried not to bark at her. "Yes?"

"One of the passengers up front has offered to switch seats with you. The bulkhead seat has extra space." She held out her other hand and tugged his elbow back toward the front of the plane.

"Oh. Uh, thanks." He swept his gaze around the plane but couldn't spot the Good Samaritan. "Who is it?" He owed them a huge thank you.

"They prefer to remain anonymous." She took his rucksack and, with surprisingly graceful strength, heaved it into the overhead compartment, which she then snapped closed. "There you go, sir." She nodded at the empty seat. Kale eyed the passengers, every single one of whom was watching him, and nodded.

"Thanks," he cast out at large. "I appreciate it."

"No, thank *you*," someone said, and applause swept through the cabin.

Kale smiled awkwardly and sat, his reaction more embarrassment than gratitude. If they knew the kinds of things he'd done in the last three years, few of them would applaud. They'd bought the line that every service member was committed to fighting for their freedom, and in so many ways they were. But the concept of dying by IED so those at home could buy giant SUVs and eat sugary breakfast cereal took it too far. They didn't know him, didn't know what he was capable of. Whether he was more worthy of a comfortable seat than the person who'd given it up.

Kale buckled his seatbelt, then sighed and closed his eyes, barely listening to the attendants' hurried preflight instructions. Forget comparing his worth to that of a random, kind stranger. The real question was if he was worthy of Amber anymore.

He didn't know. PTSD was almost a guarantee, though no one could predict how or when it would manifest. He'd saved a lot of money over the years, with no wife and kids to spend it on. His parents hadn't needed help. So he could provide financially, at least until he got himself established in a new career. He had plans for that, too. He'd have purpose and goals, things essential to adapting to civilian life.

He wasn't a statistic. But that didn't mean he couldn't add to them. Did Amber deserve that? Three years without him, much of that with no contact at all, and then suddenly she'd have to deal with his nightmares and flashbacks and bossiness.

He had to grin at that one. She definitely wouldn't take orders from him. First things first, he told himself. Get home. Surprise her. Propose in front of half the town, so the people she did so much for could give her the cheer she deserved. Then deal with what happened next, and next, and next.

And in the meantime, try to kill the terror filling him, the likes of which he'd never felt in battle.

Amber stood at the refreshment table, pouring milk for a pair of tussling brothers, when the back of her neck prickled. She straightened and looked over her shoulder at the crowded main room of the rec center. Parents and volunteers bent over kids, helping with food and crafts. Glitter dusted every surface on the far side of the room. Overall, the commotion was controlled and positive. Normal.

So why did she keep getting this sense of being watched?

Not a single pair of eyes was on her. Well, except for Rina's. She'd been a bit hovery, unconvinced that Amber was okay after last night's drinking binge.

She studied the crowd while she re-pinned the red and white hat on her head and tugged her too-short skirt a little lower. She'd either grown in all the wrong places, or was getting old. She didn't remember feeling so exposed in past years. There was an extra elf costume, but the striped tights, tunic, and hat with pointy ears just felt wrong. *If I wear this costume all day without a wardrobe malfunction…*

The sound of sleigh bells jingled over the loudspeaker, and the buzz in the room turned into excited expectation.

"Ho ho ho!" Santa strode out of the storeroom, arms wide, dragging a gigantic red and green velvet sack behind him. Amber frowned. Why was it on the floor instead of over his shoulder? Before she could do more than think the question, she was jostled by surging kids and jumped to get them organized in a line before they mobbed him. He boomed out a few more *hos* and settled his padded bulk onto the big wooden chair. The fluffy beard and wig hid almost every bit of his face, and the florescent lights reflected off the gold-rimmed glasses. No one here would be able to identify Danny, even knowing it was him under the padded costume.

His voice came over the loudspeaker now, the hearty, deep Santa version giving instructions on how the photos and gift giving were to work. That was new. Amber would have to praise his genius later, because the extra volume and reach gave authority to his words and made it easier for her and the three teenager elves to get everyone organized. Though why he announced that everyone should sit on his left knee, she had no idea.

She made sure Hannah knew how to handle the borrowed camera and printer and that Penny was ready with the candy canes. The next fifteen minutes were a whirlwind of asking kids what they were going to say to Santa, getting their whispered answers, and sending them over to him while she and Meredith found packages with the most appropriate gift for each one.

Amber was bent over the dais collecting a special present she'd set aside for one of the shelter kids when a premonition swept over her, so strong her vision went dark around the edges. *Kale.* She knew, just *knew*, that when she stood again, he'd be right there, watching her.

Her heart hammered when she slowly rose, but the space between her and the hallway entry was empty. The swinging door itself was closed, unmoving. She twisted to check the main entrance at the other end of the room. Nothing. Kids squealed and bounced as they opened presents, showing them to equally excited parents. Shreds of colorful paper littered the floor. But again, not a single person was looking at her.

She took a long, slow breath. Her fingers tightened around the package until the wrapping crinkled. *If it doesn't tear before I pass it to Santa...*

Santa's waving hand bumped her hip. Without looking down, she placed the present into it and stood still, waiting for the waves of goosebumps to stop. She felt Kale so strongly. She would have bet her *life* that he was in this room. But no matter how she scoured, how hard she looked at every face, she couldn't see anyone who could be him.

He's dead. She blinked back tears and told herself how ridiculous that was. But wasn't that how it happened? A person would see a loved one, or hear their voice, or sense them nearby, and shortly after they found out that loved one had died around that exact moment.

She had to get out of here. But there was still a steady stream of kids, and this was just the first wave. After all the festivities for the town's underprivileged, they had open Santa hours so people could get photos and kids could tell Santa what they hoped would be under the tree tomorrow morning. That part served as a fundraiser for the first part, and Amber had to be here for all of it. *If we don't run out of photo paper halfway through the second wave...*

Ten minutes later, it happened again. This time she could have sworn she smelled him. A hint of his warm, musky skin overlaid with the aftershave he'd worn the whole time she'd known him. A sob of hysteria nearly escaped her. Why was this happening? She needed to check her phone. It was in the storeroom, with her clothes, and she couldn't leave. She spun to find her cousin and spotted her hurrying up the side of the room.

"What's going on with you?" Rina whispered fiercely.

"I need my phone. Please. Back there." She waved a finger at the dark room behind them. "In my tote bag."

"Okay, fine. Calm down. I'll be right back."

But she didn't come right back. Amber grew more agitated every minute, and was just about to rush back there herself when Rina hurried out, her eyes glistening.

"What? Oh my God, what did you see?" She snatched the phone away and handed off another kid to Santa, who grunted as if he was in pain.

If there are no calls, no e-mails, no tweets... She thumbed it on and skimmed to the missed calls. Nothing.

"It's okay," Rina soothed. "There's nothing on there. No texts or anything."

Amber didn't trust her. She checked the text section, her e-mail, and Twitter and Facebook no matter how ridiculous that was. Rina was right. There was nothing there.

She dialed her home number and lifted the phone to her ear. Meredith mouthed "stuffed giraffe" at her and she sat on the second step of the dais to find it while she listened to her home phone ring and ring. No messages there, either.

"See? Everything's fine." Rina took the phone and

hurried away before Amber could confront her about the tension in her voice.

What the hell was going on?

K ale should have thought this through better.
He swallowed a moan as a kid who had to weigh a buck twenty thudded hard on his left leg. What was he, fifteen? This event had always been designated twelve and under. They were growing underprivileged kids big these days.

A half an hour ago, Kale had hidden in the dark storeroom, practically giddy with excitement that everything was coming together. The extra room in the plane had let him rest in relative comfort. He'd taken a pain pill and slept through the flight and taxiing to the gate at Boston Logan, only waking when the attendant had shaken him. The first rental car company he'd approached had a car available, and they'd given him a military discount. There'd been little traffic and no delays on his drive, and he'd arrived just before the rec center doors opened to let all the families in.

He still couldn't believe he'd sneaked in unseen—not just into the rec center, but into town, even. He'd waited in the storeroom next to the Santa outfit, hoping like hell the person who came to put it on would go along with his plan. And lo and behold, it had been his good old friend Danny.

That's when everything went to hell. Danny had walked in and closed the door, clicking on the light and reaching for the Santa suit at the same time.

"Hi," Kale had said, standing well out of reach when Danny jumped. But Danny was no soldier. He jumped back instead of forward. Watching the stream of emotion across his face stripped Kale of any happiness he'd held onto.

Shock. Dawning understanding. Joy. All expected, all

welcomed. But then despair so dark Kale had only seen it on the battlefield. Danny glanced over his shoulder, and Kale understood.

His old friend was in love with Amber. Maybe was *with* Amber. The pain of it almost sent Kale to his knees.

But then Danny hauled him into a hug, thumping him on the back. Laughing. Crying. Kale could hardly understand what the guy was saying through it all.

"Holy shit, man, she was right! I can't believe it. You're alive!"

"What?" Kale pulled back, his turn to be shocked. "What do you mean, I'm alive?"

They spent ten minutes in rapid conversation, Kale in disbelief. He'd had no idea the government had told his family he was missing. That had to be an error, but holy hell, how long had they been left like that?

His parents had decided he was dead. Thank God they were on a cruise. His surprise reappearance could have given them literal heart attacks. He hated the thought of abandoning his goal when he was so damned close to success, but maybe it would be smart.

Danny shook his head at him. "Why didn't you just walk into the rec center?"

Kale snorted. "Because I'm an asshole." He confessed his grand, romantic plan, aware his concerns were revealed in his voice.

Danny said, "She never gave up, man. She's never stopped loving you. Never stopped believing you'd be back. Go for it." And he slapped Kale hard on the right shoulder, sending a shockwave down his side. Kale doubled over, still so taken aback by everything he'd just learned that he couldn't hide his gasp of pain.

Danny came up with the speaker idea, and Kale practiced making his ho ho hos sound like his friend's. He changed into the Santa costume and dragged the bag of presents out after him, unable to lift it so much as an inch off the ground.

The whole time he'd sat here, Amber had never looked at him. A couple of times she'd acted oddly, looking around or holding very still, and Kale thought she might be on to him. But then she went on with her job. Déjà vu. That short skirt flipping around her legs, the way she bent over to get the presents—she used to do it on purpose. Kale realized Danny had watched her last year and fought off a surge of jealousy that had him squeezing the baby on his lap until it giggled as if he were tickling it.

But Kale's worries from the plane returned, and he got stuck in his fears. They were even stronger now that he knew she had no clue why he hadn't been in touch with her for so long. He sat there, listening to lisping kids rattle off their wish lists, handing them presents, staring into the flash on the camera.

Sweating. Aching. And for the first time in his life, being a coward.

Finally, he couldn't wait any longer. Every possible response had played itself out in his head, and he was close to vomiting with the weight of his inertia. The next kid was crying and pushing back against his mother, so Kale took advantage of the moment.

"Amber."

She froze halfway across the red half-circle rug. Slowly turned away from the crying child and the helpless elf trying to tug him toward Santa. Amber's eyes were huge, her mouth open a little. Kale didn't want to move, knew changing positions would make his wound scream, but he had to do this right. He levered himself rigidly off the chair and onto the floor, his left knee down. He couldn't help leaning on the right knee to take the pressure off his side, blowing out a breath of annoyance.

Amber stayed where she was, standing tall and strong and in what appeared to be complete immobility, while the room slowly went quiet around them. Kale ignored the murmured "Danny!"s and nervous throat-clearings. He slowly got his hand into his pants pocket and pulled out the ring he'd schlepped halfway across the world. Then he pulled off the Santa hat and beard. The gasp that went up made him smile, but he never took his eyes off Amber.

Fingers trembled as he tipped open the box. Amber's eyes filled with…fury. In three strides she was in front of him. He looked up, his heart in his throat.

And then she punched him in the face.

Chapter Six

"I'm sorry, I'm sorry, I'm sorry."

Dazed, Kale held himself off the floor with one hand while Amber clutched him and peppered his jaw with apologetic kisses. It was kind of funny that she thought she'd hurt him. The jaw tap wouldn't even leave a bruise, but the impact had been enough to make him twist, and the movement shot agony through his torso.

"It's okay." He'd gotten his breath back, along with a surge of relief at Amber's secondary reaction. He wrapped his free arm around her waist and straightened. Her next kiss landed on his mouth and he took immediate advantage, cupping the back of her head to hold her in place while he drugged himself with her scent. She smelled so sweet, felt so soft, tasted so amazing. He was home. *Home.*

Thunderous applause and cheering penetrated his awareness and he slowly ended the kiss but kept her close. "I'm so sorry," he whispered. "But I think I'm going to pass out."

Amber shouted for help, and Danny and some other guy

hurried over to get Kale off the floor. Amber led them outside and down the hall to an office with a sofa, and Kale let them lower him to it, as much as he wanted to stay on his feet.

"I look like a fuckin' pussy," he muttered.

"No," Danny corrected. "You look like a conquering hero. He's hurt," he told Amber. "You should get someone to look at him."

"Thanks." She dismissed the guys and turned her attention immediately to Kale's jacket, undoing it and pushing it open to examine his side. In moments, they were alone.

"This so isn't how I imagined it," Kale said. He watched her anxious eyes as she lifted his shirt and peeked under the bandage. Her hat was askew, barely held to her silky hair by some kind of pins. "I'm sorry."

"Stop apologizing." She smoothed the tape back over his ribs. "I think it's okay. It's oozing a little. Danny's right, you should see someone. But you won't die if it's not today."

Kale didn't miss the clipped tone or the roughness when she said "die." He caught her hand and pulled her off the floor to sit next to him. He had to keep her close, touching. It was so surreal to be here. The white-painted cinderblock room, with its battered, cheap metal desk and ripped-and-taped couch, wasn't unlike some field offices he'd been in. But Amber was here, tucked against him, her hands roaming up and down his torso and brushing across his face as if she, too, thought she was dreaming.

Thank God he hadn't lost her. Thank God she was still his.

"What happened to you?" she asked softly. Her hand landed on his injury, but instead of hurting, it soothed.

"I can't tell you." He pressed his mouth to the top of her head. "Bad guys. We won."

She didn't seem pleased but didn't push, either. Kale didn't fool himself that that was the end of it. She'd ask again, or about other things. She'd want to know what had filled his life while he was away from her, and he couldn't tell her much. They'd argue.

But not today.

"God, I've missed you." He couldn't hold himself back. He nudged her chin up to kiss her again. Her mouth opened immediately, letting him in, and he swept inside, reveling in her taste, her slick heat. He hardened, need pounding through his blood, and before he knew it he had her on her back on the sofa, her lush breast filling his hand.

She ripped her mouth away from his with a gasp. "Kale, we can't." But her fingers tightened in his hair and she widened her knees to cradle him. "There are kids out there. No lock on the door. They can—"

He cursed and levered himself off her. He didn't care about any of that, but he didn't want her to think he'd become an animal. Even if he felt like one.

"Sorry," he repeated. "It's been…a very long time."

"I would hope so."

He winced and gave her another apologetic look. She shifted to her knees and ran her hand through his hair again. He closed his eyes to enjoy the stroking. He never wanted it to stop. With luck, it never had to.

Wait. His eyes popped open. "Where's the ring?"

Amber's mouth dropped open in horror. "Oh my God. You dropped it when I slugged you."

Kale jumped up. "Shit. All those kids out there, someone probably pocketed it. Or stepped on it. We—" He stopped. Amber knelt on the threadbare cushion, holding the ring up at him with two fingers. "You had it all along. You little tease!"

She ignored that. "Kale Riker, you bastard. You have a lot to make up for. Will you marry me next week and get started on that, please?"

"Fuck, yeah!" He hauled her carefully into his arms and kissed her breathless again, this time making sure her hand, with the ring, was wrapped inside his so it didn't go anywhere.

They were interrupted by a knock on the door. Kale held her long enough to slip the ring on. It was loose, but Amber closed her fist to hold it in place. "Come in!" they called together.

A swarm of people flooded the office and dragged them back outside so the town could welcome Kale home. He tried to resist, but Amber nudged him into their arms, her eyes full of promise that she'd be there when he was done.

It was hours before they could break away and go home. Amber knew as soon as they walked into her little house that living in it would never work. It wasn't just Kale's size, though he seemed to fill the room and leave none for her. His force of personality had grown enormous and now took up as much space as his body did.

Amber set aside her concerns long enough to welcome him home properly, grateful that she'd stuffed the king-sized bed into her modest master bedroom because a smaller bed would have made things…well, not impossible, but definitely less magical. Kale insisted he was cleared for sex. Amber didn't believe him, but the first time took them both to the moon so quickly he didn't have time to do any further damage.

The second time took longer, but was gentler, too, and she wept when they came together, wrapped tightly around each other, expressing their love in every possible way.

Afterward, they went down to the kitchen, where Amber scrounged for enough food to cook a healthy meal while Kale tried to call his parents.

"Voice mail." He hung up her old-fashioned wall phone and reached around her to pick a carrot off the cutting board. "I don't want to leave a message. They've been through enough." He bent to kiss her and then grinned. "I can't believe I'm here. Holding you."

Amber twisted so he cradled her against his chest and kept chopping. He was so warm and solid. All the years without him seemed to shrink to minutes. "As soon as your parents are home, we need to do our Christmas dinner. It helped us through while you were gone, you know."

Kale's arm snugged around her waist, and he rocked them a little, not saying anything. She could practically feel the guilt radiating off of him. He was probably thinking of all the special events he'd missed.

The past was the past, and it didn't matter right now. Amber didn't want to spoil his homecoming with it. But she couldn't avoid the gigantic, looming question hanging over their heads any longer. "What about your commitment?" She turned to face him and toyed with his dog tags, unsure why such a simple strand of metal made a man so masculine. She wanted to hate them, what they represented, but she couldn't. "To the military?"

"I'm done," he said unequivocally, locking his hands at the small of her back.

"Really?" She didn't think it was going to be that easy. "When?"

His eyes shifted, and she sighed.

"Be straight with me."

"I'm not actually... Shit." He banged his head lightly against the cupboard behind him. "My assignments are classified. I can't give you the details you need. But I am done, Amber." He bent toward her, squeezing her hand around his tags. "My contract is terminated. I promise you."

"No more separations?"

Another eye shift, but he didn't try to evade this time. "I don't know. I've developed business plans for a consulting group, but if I follow through, it would mean traveling. I thought maybe, with your degree, you'd want to work with me. We could do it together." His eyes tracked around the kitchen, to the walls she'd filled with photos of her friends and the groups and committees she was involved with. "I don't want to take you away from what you have here, though. We'll have to—"

But Amber was so excited she couldn't stand still. She didn't need all that anymore. She could take her life off hold. "I love it. I don't need to stay in Hempfield. It would take a little time to break away, but of course I want to work with you."

He laughed. "Wait until you hear what the job is before you agree to it. I learned that lesson the hard way." He sobered. "I won't lie, it's not going to be easy. There are gonna be a ton of adjustments for both of us, and I've known guys, families, who couldn't do it."

"I know," she assured him. "The Internet is a great research tool. I'm not blind to what we're going to have to get through. But Kale…" She laid her hand on his chest and drew a breath that shuddered from the pleasure of having him here. Alive. Within reach. Everything else would follow, even if they had to wrestle it into place. "I believe in you. In us. If you believe in me…"

If he says he does…

He kissed her hand, where she'd used string to hold the ring on until she could get it sized. "I do. I promise you, I will never give up. The way you never gave up on me."

…we'll live happily ever after.

About the Author

Natalie J. Damschroder writes high-stakes romantic adventure, sometimes with a paranormal bent. Since 2000, she's published 10 novels, 7 novellas, and 14 short stories, many of them exploring magical abilities, but all with a romantic core. She currently lives in Pennsylvania with her perfect partner of a husband and two daughters who are so amazing, they've been dubbed "anti-teenagers." Learn more about her at her website, www.nataliedamschroder.com, follow her on Twitter @NJDamschroder, or like her Facebook page at / NJDamschroder.